Hawk

The Trap

Tony Reno

High Noon Books
Novato, California

Editor: Jim Arena
Cover Art: Jim McConnell
Cover Design: Bonnie Gatter
Illustrations: Jim McConnell

International Standard Book Number: 1-57128-328-5

14 13 12 11 10 09 08 07 06 05
10 09 08 07 06 05 04 03 02 01

You'll enjoy all the High Noon Books.
Write for a free full list of titles.

Contents

The Town of Point Cape

CHAPTER 1

The Surf Meet

It was a clear, sunny day. Mick and Hawk were flying over Point Cape. It was almost 10:00 a.m. and Hawk was late. He should have been at the surf meet an hour ago.

Point Cape was one of the best surf spots in the country. Hawk could see the entire beach from the plane. There were many people watching the meet. Surfers were riding waves all along the shore.

"I see a few surfers getting ready to make their run. Looks like some pretty good waves

1

today," Mick said.

Hawk looked out toward the ocean. He saw some jet-skiers and a motor-boat. They were riding close to a small island just off shore. They each had a RIVAL Extreme Sports logo on their shirts.

"What's over there?" Hawk asked, pointing toward the island. Hawk took a picture with his new under-water camera.

"Just a tiny island. There's nothing on it," Mick said.

"Then why is RIVAL going there? They are always up to something," Hawk said. "I'm glad I'm working for ACME Extreme Sports."

"No kidding," Mick said. "Speaking of

ACME, the Company Bosses will be very upset if you don't test the new board. And I don't know if you are going to get there in time to make this run."

"That's why we can't let that happen," Hawk said. "Keep flying over the waves toward the surfers."

Mick looked over at Hawk. Mick had flown planes and copters for ACME for a long time. Hawk was 21 years old. He was an extreme athlete. He had been working at ACME for a few years.

"I don't like the sound of this," Mick said.

"We don't have any other choice." Hawk reached for his ACME board. He opened the door to the plane.

"See you tonight," Hawk shouted as he jumped out of the plane. His camera was in a pocket on his belt. The surfboard fell with him.

Mick saw Hawk land in the water. He then turned the plane around. He reached for his CB radio.

"Mick to ACME, over," Mick said.

"ACME here. Boss 2 speaking," Boss Number 2 said.

"I've just dropped Hawk off," Mick said. "I need to do something before I pick him up this afternoon."

"Fine," said Boss Number 2. "Did you tell Hawk about RIVAL and the island?"

"Didn't have to," Mick said. "He saw it himself. He even took a picture. Let's hope he takes more. I know RIVAL is up to something."

CHAPTER 2

Dropping In

Hawk hit the water before the board. He had landed on the top of a wave. The other surfers had made their last run of the morning. He was the last man out. Hawk got on the board and paddled.

The crowd on the beach saw Hawk jump out of the plane. Hawk could hear the announcer say from the beach, "Looks like Hawk Davidson is here after all. And he's got a good wave. Let's see if he can handle it."

The waves at Cape Point were strong. Hawk

paddled faster. The 25-foot wave almost over-ran him. He stood up just in time.

He came off the top of the wave. He felt like he was dropping off a 15-foot ledge. For a second he felt weightless – like he was barely touching the wave.

Hawk was now in the tube of the wave. There was nothing like being in the tube. The wave took Hawk a few hundred feet down the coast.

After a few seconds, he came out of the tube. But it wasn't over. Hawk was now on another wave. It pitched up higher than the first one.

Hawk now dropped 20 feet. The wave was stronger than the first and moving fast. It threw

Hawk forward. He needed all his strength to stay on his board.

But Hawk stood firmly on his ACME board. After a few seconds, he came out of the second tube. Spray shot all around him. He could hear the crowd on the beach. They were cheering.

"Guess I did OK," Hawk said to himself.

The announcer spoke over the loud-speaker: "What a run for Hawk Davidson and ACME Extreme Sports. That puts him in third place. Trevor Howard is still in the lead. And Sam Turner, surfing for RIVAL Extreme Sports, is still in second."

"Sam's here?" Hawk said. "I should have known. Surfing is one of her better sports."

"Don't miss the last run this afternoon,"

Hawk heard over the loud-speaker. "Anything can happen here at Cape Point."

CHAPTER 3

Trevor's Surf Shop

Hawk came in from the beach. He pulled out his cell phone and called Samantha Turner. Hawk had known Sam for a few years. Like Hawk, she was very good at extreme sports. Sam told him to meet her at Trevor's Surf Shop.

"You found the place," Sam said as Hawk walked inside. It was a small shop. Surfboards, wet suits, and other gear took most of the space.

"Sam, are you here to see if you can beat me at surfing?" Hawk asked.

10

"I know I can beat you at surfing," Sam said. "Remember, I'm in second place. It's him I need to beat this afternoon."

Hawk turned around.

"How's it going, dude!" Trevor Howard said. He shook Hawk's hand.

Trevor went on, "That was some entrance, man. I'll have to try that sometime. I've done just about everything else on a surfboard."

"Trevor's a world-class surfer," Sam said. "And he owns this surf shop."

"I've heard about you. I've read about you in the surf mags," Hawk said. "I hear you also own the waves here."

"Not anymore. Nobody does now. Not

after it started going crazy," Trevor said.

"What do you mean 'crazy'?" Hawk asked.

"I mean the waves. It was nuts before, but now it's really going off," Trevor said.

"I surf here often," Sam said. "The waves have changed. They've gotten higher and stronger. Nobody knows why. Sometimes the waves are too big to surf unless they tow you out with a jet-ski."

"The surf can change. Like, when they build a pier or a break-wall," Trevor said. "I remember when they built the pier here at Cape Point. That changed the flow of the water. It made an under-water sandbar move. That made the

12

waves at the surf spot better."

"How did they know the sandbar was going to move?" Hawk asked.

"They didn't," Sam replied. "It's hard to tell how the ocean will react. Making good waves is very tough."

"People are getting better at making waves. But you have to do a lot of research first," Trevor said.

"Like what?" Hawk asked.

"Like how the currents move, and the shape of the ocean floor," Trevor answered.

"Are they building anything at Cape Point now?" Hawk asked.

"RIVAL is building a gas station. They are

also putting up a snack bar next to the RIVAL hotel," Trevor said.

"I mean in the water," Hawk said.

"Not that I know of. Nothing that would change the waves," Trevor said.

"Mick and I saw some RIVAL jet-skiers heading toward a tiny island," Hawk said. "What would they be doing out there?"

"I've seen them out there myself. Sometimes they take a motor-boat," Trevor said, "I've always wondered what they were doing. There is nothing on the island but sand and palm trees."

"I don't trust them," Hawk said, "How about you, Sam? After all, you work for them.

Have you ever been out there?"

"Hawk, you know I don't know everything that goes on at that place," Sam replied. "RIVAL sent me here to compete at the surf meet."

"Why don't you just work for ACME?" Hawk asked Sam.

"If I did that, I wouldn't be able to beat you," Sam said with a grin. "I gotta go, guys. See you for the final run this afternoon." Samantha Turner opened the door and walked out of Trevor's Surf Shop.

"What's up with you two?" Trevor asked.

"I'm not exactly sure myself," Hawk said. "Hey, do you know where I can rent a jet-ski? We've still got a couple of hours before the meet.

I want to check out that island beyond the surf."

"I rent jet-skis here. You can use one of mine, man," Trevor said. "I'd like to check it out, too. But I have to watch my shop until I surf again in the meet."

"Thanks, Trevor," Hawk said. "And good luck."

"Same to you, dude. And don't forget about The Trap."

"OK," Hawk said as he opened the door to leave. Then he stopped and turned around.

"What's The Trap?" Hawk asked

"If you surf too far down the shore, you may get stuck," Trevor replied. "It's kind of like a whirlpool. If you are not careful, you could get

16

sucked in," Trevor said.

"I never heard about this before. Mick or the ACME Bosses should have said something..."

"It just appeared a couple of months ago after the huge waves began to form here," Trevor said.

CHAPTER 4

Bagging It

It was now about noon. Hawk was cruising on Trevor's jet-ski. His ACME surfboard was with him.

"Can't forget the last part of the meet is in one hour," Hawk said to himself.

As he rode beyond the surf, Hawk could see a small island out in the ocean.

"That looks like the island Mick and I saw from the plane," Hawk said.

He sped up to full speed and headed

toward the island. The jet-ski skipped over the ocean currents. Hawk looked around. He could not see any other boats or jet-skis.

A few minutes later Hawk was nearing the island. It was small and flat with many palm trees. It would only take a few minutes to walk across the whole island.

He rode the jet-ski onto the beach and got off. He could not see the rest of the island through the palm trees. He decided to walk to the other side.

Hawk left his surfboard on the jet-ski. He took a Power Bar out of his other pocket. He also had his water-proof camera.

As he walked, he felt the hot sand on his

bare feet. Hawk wondered what RIVAL would be doing here. He did not see any buildings. Just more palm trees.

It was true – the island was small. After a couple of more minutes, he could now see the beach on the other side of the island. He looked through the trees.

Suddenly, Hawk heard the sound of engines. He stopped and ducked down. A motor-boat and two jet-skis pulled up to the beach.

Three men got off the motor-boat. They carried large white plastic bags and shovels with them. They had the RIVAL logo on their shirts.

"Bingo!" Hawk said to himself. "But what are they doing here? Looking for buried treasure?"

20

Hawk stayed down. He was a couple hundred feet from the men.

The two jet-skiers joined the three from the motor-boat. The five men started putting sand into the white bags. Hawk watched as they filled about 50 bags. They then hauled them to the boat.

Hawk crawled until he got a clear view. Then he took a picture. The men got on the boat and started the engine.

"Shoot," said Hawk. "I've got to get to the jet-ski and follow them." He crawled back behind the trees and ran to the other side of the island.

After a few minutes of running, Hawk was breathing hard. He made it back to his jet-ski. He looked out at the water, but he could not see the motor-boat and the jet-skiers.

"Excuse me, I think they went that way," a voice said.

Hawk turned around. He saw a man in a grey business suit.

"What?" Hawk said. He was surprised to see the man.

"The motor-boat and the jet-skiers. I think they went back to the surf at Cape Point," said the man.

"Thanks," said Hawk.

"No problem," said the Grey Man. "Don't forget to take more pictures."

"I gotta go," Hawk said.

"I know," said the Grey Man. "RIVAL vs.

ACME. Do you ever feel like you are being pulled between them?"

"What do you mean?" asked Hawk,

"I thought you were here for the surf meet," the Grey Man said.

"I am," said Hawk.

"Then why are you chasing RIVAL?" the Grey Man asked.

"I don't have time for this," Hawk pushed the jet-ski into the water. He started the engine.

"There are other choices. Think about it," said the Grey Man. He opened his briefcase. "Sign a contract with me and I can offer you instant fame."

"I'll stick with ACME," Hawk said.

"Nobody's perfect, but they are better than RIVAL."

"If you insist. I admire your loyalty," the Grey Man said.

Hawk began to drive away.

"Bye, Hawk. Maybe we will see each other again."

CHAPTER 5

Making Waves

Hawk found the motor-boat and the two RIVAL jet-skiers. They stopped before the surf at Cape Point. They were still far from the beach. It was hard for anyone on the beach to see them.

Hawk was behind them. He stayed a few hundred feet away. Two men in the boat put on scuba gear. They then rolled off the boat into the water. The driver of the motor-boat gave a sandbag to each diver. The divers went under the water.

Hawk was puzzled. What could they be

doing with bags of sand? He decided to get a closer view. He got into the water with his water-proof camera and swam. He held his breath and dove down. The water was very clear.

Hawk was next to a white reef. It went on for hundreds of feet. There were many fish around it. The divers were ahead. Hawk took an under-water picture. The divers put the bags onto the reef. Hawk took another picture. The divers then went up to the surface.

Then Hawk saw that the white reef was really hundreds, maybe thousands, of white bags. He snapped one more photo. He was running out of breath. He went back to the surface.

"RIVAL is shaping the surf," Hawk said to

Then Hawk saw that the white reef was really hundreds, maybe thousands, of white bags.

himself as he gulped for air. "Better get those pictures to Trevor. He will know what to do with them." He swam to Trevor's jet-ski.

When Hawk was on his jet-ski, he looked back at the motor-boat. The three men in the boat were looking at Hawk. One of them started the engine of the motor-boat.

"They saw me." Hawk started his motor and headed away from them. Then he remembered, "I'm late for the second part of the surf meet. I have to get back there!"

CHAPTER 6

Tubular Session

The RIVAL divers were surprised to see Hawk turn around. He would have to pass them to make it to the surf meet.

Hawk watched the other two men get back in the water. They did not have their scuba gear on. Instead they had special surfboards with grips for their feet. Each held onto a rope. Each rope was tied to a jet-ski.

The motor-boat started to move away. The two jet-skiers each towed a diver.

Hawk passed right by them.

"Give us your camera, Hawk, and we won't hurt you," the driver shouted from the boat.

Hawk kept heading for the surf meet. The meet was just a few hundred yards down the coast.

Hawk could hear the announcer on the beach say over the loud-speaker: "What a run by Sam Turner and RIVAL Extreme Sports! That puts her in a tie with Trevor Howard. Too bad Hawk Davidson is not here for the final run."

The surfers were going in for the day. The waves were higher than this morning. The water was now moving too fast. The surfers could not paddle fast enough to catch the waves.

"Just like Trevor said. The surf's really going off," Hawk said to himself. "But the ACME Bosses will be angry if I don't finish the meet."

Hawk was coming up to the surf meet. The waves looked like they were 80 feet high.

The RIVAL jet-skiers had swung around and were now behind Hawk. But the motor-boat was faster than the jet-skis. At that second, the motor-boat pulled up next to Hawk.

"This is your last chance, Hawk," yelled the RIVAL driver. "Give us the camera, or we will take it from you!"

At the same time a huge wave began to swell under him. It lifted Hawk up like an elevator. He kept going as fast as he could on his jet-ski.

Hawk was now between the waves and the motor-boat. The jet-skiers towing the divers were right behind him. The motor-boat tried to bump Hawk's jet ski. He had no choice but to turn into the waves.

Hawk grabbed his surfboard with one hand. Then he let out a yell and dove off his jet-ski. He flew over the top and down the face of the wave. While he was still in the air, he pulled the board in under his legs. The board and Hawk both skimmed down the surface of the wave. He must have dropped 50 feet. It almost felt as if he were skiing.

Hawk heard the voice on the loud-speaker: "Folks, it looks like the meet isn't over quite yet.

It seems that Hawk Davidson has made another awesome entrance!"

The fast wave shot Hawk through the tube. Foam was spraying everywhere. Hawk could not believe he had made it.

Hawk looked back for a second. One of the jet-skiers had crashed on the wave. The guy he was towing also went down. But the other jet-ski had made it through and was still behind Hawk.

Then the voice on the loud-speaker said: "Hawk had better watch out! If he keeps going he's in for a surprise."

"What's he talking about? What else could happen?" Hawk wondered.

Hawk grabbed his surfboard with one hand.
Then he let our a yell and dove off his jet-ski.

Just then Hawk rode into another wave that threw him forward. He flew off his board into the ocean. The camera also went in with him.

CHAPTER 8

The Trap

Hawk was now stuck in a swirling mass of currents. He did his best to stay above water. The waves kept pulling him down.

This must be The Trap that Trevor was talking about, thought Hawk.

Hawk was having a hard time getting free. The waves would hold him down for 20 seconds or longer. The ocean currents were not bringing him out of The Trap. Hawk thought he could hear the announcer on the beach talking about him.

But Hawk was too busy trying to stay alive. Another wave sucked him down again. It felt like he was in a washing machine. This time something hit him. He couldn't see under water, but he reached out. It was the camera.

Just then he felt something pull at the camera. It was the RIVAL diver. He had let go of the rope to the jet-ski and followed Hawk into The Trap. Hawk and the RIVAL athlete wrestled for the camera. Another wave pulled them down under water for 15 seconds.

"For the last time, Hawk. Give us the camera," said the RIVAL athlete. Then another wave pulled them down again.

I can't take much more of this, Hawk

thought to himself.

Suddenly, a jet-ski appeared next to Hawk.

"Hang in there, Hawk," yelled a female voice.

"Sam?" Hawk asked.

Another wave crashed down next to Sam. She was no longer there.

"Sam! Sam! Where are you?!" Hawk yelled.

Then, out of the spray and mist, Sam's jet-ski appeared. She swung around next to Hawk.

"Grab on, Hawk," said Sam.

Hawk grabbed onto her jet-ski. Sam then pulled Hawk out of The Trap and took him into calm waters.

"Grab on, Hawk," said Sam. Hawk grabbed onto her jet-ski.

"I'm going back for the RIVAL guy," Sam said.

Hawk was out of breath but glad to be alive. He had the camera. He did not know where his ACME board had gone. It went under water and never came back up.

Hawk began to swim to the shore. Then he heard the noise of boat engines. He turned around. The RIVAL motor-boat was coming his way. Hawk was still several hundred feet to the beach. He tried to swim fast, but he was too tired.

CHAPTER 9

And the Winner Is . . .

The RIVAL motor-boat pulled up next to Hawk. There were four men inside.

"I guess you win," said Hawk.

"I don't think so, dude. That was one awesome run. I just heard they made you the winner," said the man in the boat.

Hawk could not believe it. There was Trevor with a few other local surfers. They pulled Hawk onto the motor-boat and headed to shore.

"What happened? I don't get it," Hawk said.

"After Sam and I surfed in the meet, we saw that you were late. You told me you were going out to the island. My surf friends and I took jet-skis out to look for you. We found the motor-boat and the driver hiding on the other side of the island. Then we came back here to find you."

"What about Sam?" Hawk asked.

"Sam decided to stay around the shore to look for you. Lucky for you. The Trap can be deadly. It can suck you down like a whirlpool," Trevor said.

"Well, now we know what makes The Trap so deadly. I have the proof right here," Hawk said. He showed his camera.

Just then Mick walked up. "Well done,

42

Hawk. Mind if I take that?" He grabbed the water-proof camera from Hawk. "RIVAL was trying to make the waves bigger so more people would come here," Mick said.

"Some people like to surf huge waves, but to surf them you need to be towed into the waves by a jet-ski," Trevor said.

"But they didn't do enough research," Mick added. "They didn't know the waves would change this much, or that the currents would become risky.

"Once RIVAL made the waves bigger, they were hoping more surfers would come to Cape Point. Then they could slowly take over the town by putting up hotels and other things," Trevor said.

"Well, after the town sees these photos, I bet they won't be letting RIVAL do anything else at Cape Point," Hawk added.

Just then Mick's cell phone rang.

"Excuse me, guys," he said. He walked a few feet away and answered his phone.

"Mick here," he said.

"This is ACME Boss 2. What happened?" the caller said.

"Mission complete," Mick said. "RIVAL won't be making trouble at Cape Point any more."